About the Author

J.S. Veter has been mainlining science fiction and fantasy since long before it was cool. She embraces her geekdom by writing more of it. Jessica is the author of three novels and has published short stories in *Beneath Ceaseless Skies*, *Luna Station Quarterly*, *New Realm*, and Seventh Star Press' anthology *Thunder on the Battlefield: Sword*.

For updates and free stories, please sign up for Jessica's newsletter at **jessicaveter.com**

the eyes have it

Other books by J.S. Veter

Gateway

Six

the eyes have it

Printed in the United States of America
First Printing, 2016
ISBN 978-0-9952283-4-4 (paperback)
ISBN 978-0-9952283-5-1 (electronic book)

Shoestring House Inc.
85 Creighton Rd.
Dundas, Ontario, Canada

www.shoestringhouse.ca

Cover image: Titima Ongkantog via Shutterstock

the
eyes
have
it

js veter

shoestring
house

2016

the eyes have it

What the heck.

This one's for me.

the eyes have it

Jay's first set of eyes (not including the ones he'd been born with) had come as part of a bulk discount at Giant Tiger. They were a gift from Jay's grandmother, an impulse purchase, something she'd not okayed with Jay's folks.

Jay's da, in the spirit of 'waste not, want not', booked him into a biotech clinic the next day. Once the puking stopped and the headaches faded, Jay returned to school to find his updates sixteen weeks out of date. The new download meant three more days of nausea.

It was worth every heave.

The matte surfaces of the classroom walls -- deliberately blank so as not to interfere with the VR displays projected by the classroom emitter -- erupted at once into vibrant colour. The day's lessons floated just behind the teacher's desk and with a blink, Jay transferred them to the memory core in his new left eye. Mr. Sparling's lecture was helped along by a 3D projection of the problem, and that was made bearable by the lewd caricature of Mr. Sparling that Lee Brown had hacked into the emitter.

On the walk home, Jay suspected the parental control settings on his eyes were 18+. The Victoria's Secret model splayed across the hood of a car parked on Goring Avenue confirmed it. She also confirmed a few more things Jay had been wondering about since starting middle school.

But the eyes were glitchy: system upgrades tended to tunnel vision and, eventually, UV faded the right iris from deep brown to a kind of dog-poop yellow.

Jay spent three years saving up for his second set: high-rez, suped-up 220 gig, 1500 pix baby blues capable of storing the equivalent of fifty digitized Libraries of Congress. They came with instant capture-and-send, their own 3D emitter and built in 15G. Jay had them installed on his fifteenth birthday, spent ten days in bed waiting for his flesh to stop battling his tech, then returned to school to find that OIC had introduced a wetware system which made Jay's hardware obsolete.

By the time he was twenty, Jay's baby blues were quaintly retro.

By the time he was twenty-two, Jay's 15G system could no longer support even the slowest bandwidth. Streets and public buildings faded to uniform matte grey as Jay and others like him were excluded from net advertising and cloud entertainment broadcasts.

When Jay was twenty-five, Logicorpus lost the suit which would have forced OIC to make its wetware tech back-compatible with Logicorpus' now unfashionable biotech. People were left with no choice but a pricey upgrade to wetware, staggering environmental disposal fees and test-tube eyebuds (which may or may not 'take'; the human brain became stubbornly less adaptable after puberty). Black-market biotech upgrades were a cheaper option, but even those were out of Jay's price-range these days. There was a third option (cheaper still, and illegal as hell), but the gross-out factor was a bit of a hurdle.

For a time.

*

"How we doing?" Skye had wiggled a paper clip between the wall and the elevator's control panel, popped the cover off and now pressed one end of the clip into the hold button.

"Fourth floor." Jay was listening at the door of the reluctantly ascending elevator. "Fifth. We should have taken the stairs."

"No way," Skye said. "I told you: we get stuck in the stairwell, we'll never get out. No one ever uses the stairwell. Remember that guy last year?"

Jay grunted. Sounds from the eighth floor faded and were replaced by the ninth: music, cutlery ringing against plates.

"He was in there, what, three days? Four? Geez. He could have died," Skye said. "How we doing?"

"Eleven."

12

"You'd think, seeing as how Holdings hired us, they'd at least install an A.I. that recognises biotech," Skye said. Skye said this every day.

"Yep," Jay said. "Or put us on the first floor. Thirteen."

"It's discrimination, I tell you," Skye said. "I hate it here. Did I tell you..."

"... I have a degree?" They laughed at the old joke. Friends by circumstance, ten years ago they'd have had nothing to say to one another. Skye joked that he leaned so far left he walked on an angle. Jay had voted big 'C' Conservative, back when he still had the vote.

The lights went out.

"Shit," Skye said. His paper clip had slipped off the hold button. The elevator, it's A.I. not recognizing the outdated biotech Jay and Skye carried, powered down, assuming it was empty. The fan slowed and stopped.

"This bites," Skye complained. "You know how long I had to wait for a bus this morning? Forty-five minutes! Finally, this woman comes along and flags the bus down for me. Tells me it's her good deed for the day."

"The bank machine stopped recognizing my thumb print last week," Jay said, slumping to the floor. "I had to go in and give a DNA sample, can you believe it? Then the bastard charges me a thirty-dollar service fee for the verification. I should have closed my account."

"Yeah, but where would you find another bank?"

"Yeah." They waited in the dark.

It wasn't the first time they'd been stuck in an elevator, nor was it the first time someone had stopped a bus for them. Wetware had been incorporated into everything these days and now that OIC had developed a bug-free A.I. template, corporations were upgrading their security systems at record pace. It was all SIM-recognition, Wifi-to-Wifi and zips.

Jay took out his emergency LED and flicked it on. Skye had settled across from him. He was pulling protein bars out of his bag. "I meant to tell you," he said. "Temp had it done."

"Really?"

"I told you, yeah? Temp heard about this guy so she went to see him. He had some 'ware for her, and she had the replant done."

"Yeah? And?"

"It's great," Skye said. "No problems."

"Seriously?" Jay's skin crawled. The first he'd heard about the replant procedure was a couple of years ago, when newsbytes of black market wetware were going around. The reports had been vague, but the net rumours were not. Bodies were being stolen and their 'ware harvested, presumably to be installed in some poor slob who couldn't afford off-the-shelf. The government had responded by slapping a crap law on the practice; making it illegal was so much faster and easier than going through the trouble of regulation. Jay followed the rumours (he had an interest) and Skye had confirmed them. That was the nice thing about Skye: in spite of his handicap, he was still one of those guys who knew a guy who knew a guy.

the eyes have it

"I made an appointment with the guy," Skye said, voice dropping.

Jay waited for the punchline. None came. "You're kidding?"

Skye shook his head, waving his hands over his head to indicate the elevator, the building, the general suckiness of life without 'ware. "Why am I putting up with this? Why are any of us? There could be a war declared tomorrow and everyone would know about it except you and me... and the other ten of us."

"3.7 percent," Jay said. It was a guess. No one really knew exactly how many people didn't have wetware. StatsCan didn't bother keeping track. "What about, you know, the donor?"

"He don't need them anymore. What do I care?"

"You're not worried about getting caught?"

"So what? The government's wrong on this. Privacy my ass. Everyone's having it done."

"You're not worried about side effects?"

"Those stories are all zipbait, Jay."

So," Jay said, "when are you getting it done?"

Skye grinned. "Next week, buddy. I've got some holiday time accrued. When I get back, all this will be over."

"Well," Jay said, "I'm happy for you, I really am." Which was a total lie, of course. Once Skye updated, Jay would be the only one in the company left with biotech. Talk about lonely.

Skye handed over a protein bar. "Hey, don't worry, buddy. I'll help you out. We can meet in the lobby every morning. I'll make sure you're okay."

The elevator started to move. Downwards.

"Right," Skye said, getting to his feet. "Whoever gets on, I don't care if it's God, is taking us up to 23 first." The lights flickered on and the fan came to life. "I'm sick of being invisible. You should get it done, you really should. I can give you this guy's number, if you want."

"How much?"

Skye told him.

Jay mentally counted his savings. He almost had enough.

*

Once Skye had returned to work with a spanking new system and a new batch of friends just a zip away, Jay knew he'd get a replant done, gross-out factor or no. Skye gave Jay Karim's number (with codes so convoluted that Jay suspected his call had rebounded over half the globe before it landed in Karim's inbox), and Skye did, actually, keep his promise of meeting in the lobby for a good two weeks before forgetting Jay existed.

It was a long haul of all-work-no-play for Jay to come up with enough money for the procedure. Finally, an inevitable string of piss-offs on the pedways brought Jay to a brownstone in Parkdale where he was introduced to Karim and a pair of organic wetware – good as new.

Skye had told Jay that Karim had been part of OIC's initial crowd-funding. If true, Karim couldn't have been more than twelve at the time, but the top-of-the-line mercury sheen across his eyes said that business was good. No nasty second-hand orbs for Karim Nadir, no sir, but he offered them to Jay without hesitation.

"At this price, someone else will snatch them up if you don't."

"It's just... you know, they're used," Jay said. Admittedly, he'd never given much thought to what had happened to his old systems when he upgraded. Had some poor kid gotten stuck with a right eye the colour of dog poop?

Jay looked at the specs again. Way better than what he had, obviously. He couldn't help but feel a bubble of excitement. The tech was less than three months old, they'd been completely sterilized and refurbished, and Karim had added a number of improvements of his own.

"I'm especially proud of the snoop," Karim said.

Jay dragged his attention back to the No Name pickle jar waiting on the table in front of him. "I nabbed it from CSIS," Karim continued. "It's not a bad little system, and the carrier is good. I added my own special mojo and poof, you get eyes as good as if you'd grown them yourself."

"What about the donor?" Jay asked.

"Took immaculate care of them. I have the anti-v certificate... here it is. He upgraded regularly via neural interface – and he was a 'he', if that kind of thing bothers you."

Jay hadn't thought about that at all.

"I've draino'd all the old files, of course, though most of those self-deleted at the point of death; no passwords, no programs running in the background, no images, no vid. Preferences a little heavy on politics for my taste, but, you know, it takes all sorts."

"Is there any chance of them being tracked?" Jay asked. He'd read about that somewhere.

Karim shook his head. "I ran them through a high-rez duplicate scanner. It came up 0/0, so I went all the way with these lovelies: tore them right down to the basics and built them up again using your DNA. Safe as houses, buddy."

"How did the donor... you know?"

Karim shrugged. "Maybe he got sick, maybe his wife found him in bed with another woman, what do you care? He doesn't need this sweet pair anymore, and you, buddy, are definitely not made of money." Karim leaned in. "Listen, man," he said, "give 'em a go. You don't like 'em, we can re-install those retro blues, for a small fee, of course. But I guarantee you won't be disappointed. I already ran your code through them. They love you. You say 'jump', they'll say 'how high'? It's like they were made for you."

Jay picked up the jar containing the eyes. The jar was a bit scuffed, the solution inside slightly cloudy. One of the eyeballs, balanced delicately on filaments of nano-connectors and quantum nerve tendrils, wobbled around to check him out. Jay looked back, wondered what it would be like to look into a mirror and have these eyes staring right back at him. They were a fashionable shade of purple, which he liked, and the system allowed for up to three hundred other shades, with colour-mixing options and the ability to pre-set instant profiles depending on the time of day and activity. There was even a setting for heterochromia, which had become wildly popular since Bowie Base One had launched last spring. When Jay got his baby blues, this tech had barely been a wet dream. So what they were used? They meant entry back into the human race. No more charity status. No more sitting in a stagnant elevator.

"How do you get them?" he asked. Skye had said something about a boyfriend who worked in a morgue. Jay tried to think of other people who had ready access to the recently dead. Karim looked like the kind of guy who might know ethically casual police officers, or paramedics.

Karim looked disgusted. "You ask questions like that, buddy, we go no further. Don't you know anything?"

Jay stumbled an apology.

"You either want them or you don't," Karim said. "You're nervous, fair enough, but if you don't take them, I'll have to scrub your DNA from their memory and that will be the last you see of your deposit."

Last week Jay's building had upgraded its security. Now when he wanted access to his own apartment he had to buzz the super to come let him in. Mr. Weiss was good about it, but Jay was sick of being invisible. It had taken Jay two hours to get here. Fifteen minutes of that time was spent waiting for someone else to join him at the pedway gate. Taxis refused to pick him up because they only accepted squirts.

Fuck being a charity case.

"Okay," Jay said, and pressed his thumb to the pad Karim offered. The machine protested 'file not found'.

"This'll be that last time you have to do this," Karim said as Jay punched his account information into the key pad from memory and added a small DNA sample as confirmation. "In two weeks, after the usual adjustments, you'll be up and running."

Jay knew what the usual adjustments were: . blindness, blurred vision, headaches and disorientation as

23

the new system took hold. "So when do we do this?' he asked.

"Now, buddy," Karim said. The money cleared Jay's account, bounced through a few dog-and-pony show servers and landed into one of Karim's many ghost accounts.

"Um, okay," Jay said, and pressed his hands between his legs.

Karim handed the pickle jar over. "You bring these, I'll go wash up."

*

"You backed up?"

Jay nodded. His stomach turned in on itself. They'd gone into another room and Jay was sitting on a plastic-covered surgical chair. Karim puttered about, and Jay, left holding the jar with his new/used eyes, watched the liquid tremble in his grasp.

"When the last time you were off-line?"

"Um, conscious? Not since I was eight," Jay said.

"Use memory a lot, or are you Old School?"

The Old School movement was a softer form of what, in its extreme, was the Naturals movement. People who were Old School actually memorized things -- numbers, URLs, the words to songs. Some actually read text rather than simply downloading. Naturals believed mankind was diminished from what it had been before the Cloud made thinking something that took place outside their grey matter. Naturals eschewed any implanted tech.

Obsolete biotech made some Old School inevitable, but, for the most part, Jay had dumped pretty much everything he had in what little Cloud access was available to his system.

"I'll be okay," Jay said, handing the jar to Karim and leaning back. He didn't relish being offline, but it was a price he was willing to pay.

"Some people panic," Karim said, pointing at the straps hanging off the side of the chair. "It's just a precaution." He tied Jay's right hand down and pulled the strap tight. It was hard not to panic. Karim tied Jay's left hand down, and then, even worse, he secured a strap across Jay's chest. Another went across his forehead.

Karim placed a quick drive, which he'd plugged into a small think box, beside Jay's head. "Don't worry, I've made it back compatible, and I'll do a once over before we shut you down. Go."

Jay told his baby blues to send the entire contents of his antique drive into the think box. Jay watched the icon in his right eye blink at him in a kind of panic. This was the easy part, just making another copy so Karim could clean any bugs out of it and download it into the new system. It took less than a minute to upload the entire contents of the last ten years' of Jay's life (plus whatever he'd saved from his first system) to the think box.

"You're good," Karim said. "Power down."

That was just an expression. There was no power, per se, just a small circuit that ran off the not-insignificant magnetic field a person generated simply by living. Jay took a deep breath.

"Okay," he said, and hit the switch. For the first time since he was a kid, Jay went off-line.

His system complained, Jay confirmed the command, and the system wailed its protest. Jay held still, pushed down the panic impulse that wanted him to toggle the 'abort' sequence. And then it was done. Karim watched Jay's Wifi go dark.

"Good for you," he said. "That's the worst bit."

Jay blinked, vision fading to shades of blue and green as the receptors in his eyes tried to get hue and saturation just right. It was like forgetting colours, and then it was like forgetting light, and then Karim's voice was moving away from him.

"That should take pretty quickly," Karim seemed to say, and the last thing Jay remembered thinking was that he must have been drugged; of course he'd been drugged, or else how would Karim take his baby blues from his head without Jay giving a damn at all?

SYSTEM DOWN

REBOOT.

REBOOT FAILED.

There had been a time when Jay had been a Natural.

He'd never thought of it quite like that before; the term hadn't existed in the modern sense when it could have been used to describe Jay. But, there had been a time when the only memory he'd had in his head was what nature had given him. He vaguely remembered an old laptop computer sitting on the kitchen counter in his parents' house. Man, when was the last time Jay had seen a laptop?

Jay felt pressure as if from a distance. There was a sucking sound. He felt a touch on his face. The sensation was odd, unaugmented by tags which could have told him temperature, pressure, bacteria count and all the other app info he was used to getting.

Jay tried to follow what was being done to him. He had a vague feeling he might need the information for later, but without his tech, his thinking was fuzzy and disorientated. A sudden wash of cool descended over Jay, and there was an opening, and then a sharp stab of pain. Jay knew he'd made a sound, though he'd promised himself he wouldn't, and then there was nothing for a long time, no data coming to him at all, and it might have gone on for a minute or a hundred years.

Then a flash like lightening, and the sound of roaring and a crack resounded through his skull. There was pain. Pain! Something had hit him. Something huge and hard.

"Whoa! Whoa!"

Hands on him, holding him down, and the stink of vomit and the strap across his forehead was torn away so suddenly his neck snapped forward.

"Shit, Jay, it's all right!" Karim's voice, that was, and Jay flailed, his arms still secured but his feet were free and one foot connected with something that crashed metallically.

"What's with him?" someone asked.

"Shadow-file," Karim said. "I'll have to put him out."

29

the eyes have it

And then there was nothing.

Nothing at all.

*

"We're at your place."

It was Asif, a long-time friend and the 'emergency contact' Jay had given Karim.

"Don't."

Jay let his hands drop.

"You really went nuts, man," Asif said. "You should see what you did to Karim's place. I didn't know you had it in you."

"What happened?" Jay's hands drifted to his face again. Asif let him explore the bandage over his eyes. It was less than he'd expected. The skin above and below the bandage was numb. His sinuses ached. "Something hit me."

"I don't think so. There was something in the new system he missed when he booted it up. It's gone now, but you sure as hell didn't like it." Something touched Jay's lips. A straw. Jay took a drink of water and let his head fall back. He was sure he'd been hit. He remembered... lights. Lights and a sensation of falling. But, other than his sinuses, he felt fine.

"When can I login?" Jay said.

"Anytime," Asif said. "Everything's there, and Karim says you've got the bootcode."

Jay licked his lips. His bladder clenched.

"Login already!" Asif said "I've got four years' worth of shit I can't wait to zip you."

Jay grinned blindly and spoke his bootcode.

*

"Good morning, Mr. Chadha," the Holdings A.I., nicknamed Alice, murmured in his ear, swinging the building's door open as he approached. "I have set your cubicle at your preferred temperature of 21 degrees. I note you're running a little late and assume you didn't have time for coffee. Shall I have some waiting for you?"

"Yes, please," Jay subvocalized. "And open my calendar for today." His itinerary blossomed in front of him.

The elevator opened as he approached. Jay didn't even have to change his pace. God, he loved this. Sure, there had been some issues since he'd had the replants installed. His personal preferences kept switching on him, for some reason. This morning he'd been awakened to some All-Classical feed, the other day his neighbourhood adboards had displayed nothing but diet supplements. And he still had that vague, niggling sinus headache. Pain killers kept it under control, but he could still feel it, a shadow behind his eyes. Thankfully, his system was fine; it was just as if a stranger had crashed at his place while he was away.

Jay's violet eyes flicked through a series of employee memos, helpfully displaying and then saving the ones relevant to Jay's department. His system automatically added meetings and appointments to his itinerary and set notifications. Jay stepped off the elevator at his floor and entered his cubicle, where a steaming extra-large coffee, double-double, waited in his dispenser. He sat in his chair, and his system, registering that he was safely seated, sent him his daily hits. His personal settings were adjusted to news and entertainment, heavy on the entertainment, and today's news was all about Bridgette's marriage and subsequent divorce (twenty minutes later) from all three of her wives. Zips were fast and furious. Jay came across several handles he knew and zipped their comments on to his own circles. His last zip had garnered him seventeen new followers since breakfast. He tagged them and his system auto-checked them against known troll and phishing idents. Two were clean and shared 87 per cent or higher on his 'interests' scale, so he followed them back.

Which is when it happened again. There was a blip, and a scrolling newspaper appeared at the bottom of his POV: *Prime Minister to lead 36th Annual Climate Change Response Conference…. Pedway accident decapitates pensioner during mid-week peak…. Peter James Anderson missing since 3/17. Feds fear foul play…. ISS orbit continues to degrade, ESA waffles.* Jay suffered through six more news items before he got his settings up and changed back to his defaults.

In spite of that, however, things were really looking up. Jay had three new badges on his virtual cubicle and received a new ream of contact information in his queue. He had been points' leader three hours in a row on Monday, and everyone knew how hard it was to do that on a Monday.

And the new girl in the cubicle next to his, Sandra, had zipped him on her first day and he'd zipped her right back. Then they'd talked on Holdings' public forum. Someday soon, Jay promised himself, he was going to say 'hi' to her in person.

Jay took his coffee and flipped through his messages: a reminder from Asif that they were getting together for lunch, two missed calls from his father, a going-away party for Skye and a zip from someone named Billy. Jay tapped the zip and it opened, but it was just a poke, no personal message. Jay asked Alice to find out who sent the zip, answered Asif's reminder with a 'See You Then!", and sent his father an automated call-back.

"Sorry, Mr. Chadha," Alice said. Her voice, really a digital signal sent via the aural connectors attached to his new eyes, was apologetic. "I have no Billy on file with that I.P. location. I have cross-referenced with municipal and provincial databases, private and public, but have found no links. Would you like me to request Federal access?"

"God, could you imagine the forms?" Jay said, rubbing the bridge of his nose. It was time for another painkiller. "No thanks." If it was important, this Billy, whoever he was, would try him again.

At nine o'clock on the dot, Jay's screen came down and his stats page came up. His numbers were still up, but Jay knew that. He'd been top of the board eighteen hours straight, reaching this apex only six days after recovering from his replant. It felt good. It felt fucking amazing, to be honest, and not for the first time he told himself that that visit to Karim had been the best money he'd ever spent, headache or no.

the eyes have it

Jay swallowed two tablets with the last of his coffee and asked Alice to begin. Jay's system, connected to Holdings' server since he'd entered the building, accessed the queue dump that had been waiting, and sent its first request of the day. Somewhere in Asia, Chan Lin Yao's eyes told him he had a call coming in and he answered.

"Good evening, Mr. Chan," Jay said, and Alice translated Jay's English into flawless Mandarin. "My name is Jay and I'm calling for Holdings PLC on behalf of Paneurasia Telecom. Permission to initiate video link?"

*

Jay met Asif at a coffee pub down the street from Holdings. The scanner at the door took his personal preferences, downloaded his friends list, sent out invitations to those friends to join Jay, and had his choice of beverage waiting at what the A.I. calculated was a table which matched Asif and Jay's needs most exactly, given individual preferences and desires. As Jay passed under the arch, the pub's A.I. deducted a small service fee from his bank account along with the cost of two coffees and a butter tart that appeared in the dispenser as they sat down. Asif set his tags to public and left his inbox wide open.

"You look... different," Asif said, looking Jay up and down. "Got a date?"

Asif and Jay had worked in neighbouring cubicles for three years until Asif had saved enough to get his wetware installed. His left eye had grown wrong, however, leaving it vague and milky. Asif said its reception was excellent, but its broadcast, however, was iffy. Asif had been forced to leave Holdings when Alice had been installed; the A.I. had registered him as a virus and attacked his system. Now, Asif worked freelance for a number of smaller companies who didn't care that he worked from home.

Jay adjusted the collar of his shirt self-consciously. "I don't look like a zek, do I?"

"No, no," Asif said. "Nothing like a zek, just... not used to seeing you in a shirt with buttons."

37

the eyes have it

"I need to do laundry," Jay said. Which was true, but not an excuse for the collared shirt, which he'd not worn since graduation five years ago. Truth, he'd pulled a clean-enough t-shirt out of the hamper this morning and suddenly it hadn't been right. Jay hadn't liked the way it hung from his shoulders, it made him feel all angles and wrong-jointed. The buttoned shirt, hanging in the back of his closet, had been a 'why not?' experiment, and he'd liked it. He'd even put on a belt.

A woman walked past their table. Asif shifted, and Jay guessed he'd zipped her. She was Asif's type: small and dark and glittering with 'ware. She carried her own emitter around her neck, and broadcast her refusal of Asif's invitation all over their table. Jay laughed out loud.

"Ouch," Asif said, but he wasn't that upset. Three people in the pub who thought the woman's refusal harsh immediately sent him zips of their own. Then, the pub arch pinged a warning.

"Check that out," Asif said. A woman had come into the pub, and the arch, not getting a reading from her system, raised the alarm.

"Shit," Jay said. "Are those real?"

"I think so," Asif said. "Zip her, I dare you!"

Jay couldn't have been the only one who tried it. Feeling a bit self-conscious, he zipped the woman. It was like dropping a stone into a bottomless pit.

"Holy crap," Asif said, having sent his own zip. The pub A.I. must have sent a warning to the manager, because there was a flurry of activity at the back and then a ware-heavy man wearing a name tag showed up. The woman, who Jay thought might have been pretty if not for the flat, depthless look to her unaugmented eyes, stepped back as the pub manager intercepted her. They had a tense conversation: the woman gesturing to the people in the pub, the manager blocking her entrance.

"I've never seen a Natural before," Asif said.

"Me neither," Jay said, watching her. She was enviously easy in her skin. Jay had hated being invisible, yet there was this woman, walking around without a single piece of tech in her person as if it were the most normal thing in the world. "I feel sorry for her," he said. "She doesn't know what she's missing." The woman finally relented: the pub was 'ware only. The manager wouldn't accept payment by thumbprint, DNA sample nor even, had the woman been so crass as to suggest it, cash money. She left. Jay thought she had guts, the way she walked away without even once looking back.

All at once it was worth it: the screwy system preferences (which today kept switching to Premier League Football for some reason), the headaches, even the nausea. Jay didn't even care anymore that his eyes were replants. They were his, now. That Natural was not him, never would be him, ever, and he would never have anyone feeling sorry for him ever again. Jay punched Asif in the shoulder, harder than he should have, probably, but his heart was pounding with possibility.

Jay's system pinged. It was another zip from that frigging Billy. That made the fourth time today. Who the hell was this guy? Jay, buzzing with adrenaline, had had enough. He told his system to block Billy.

And Jay's eyes shut him down.

Jay cried out, grabbing for the table. But he had no input, nothing. No tactile, no aural, no visual. His entire system had crashed.

SYSTEM UPGRADE IN PROCESS.

REBOOTING.

The house looms behind him. There's something lying under the hedgerow. Then lights. Falling. CRACK! and silence.

PLEASE WAIT FOR START MENU.

Jay was flooded with light and sound. The upgrade took hold, making the room spin.

"Jay!" Asif exclaimed. "You okay? You've, um, made a bit of a mess."

Jay had puked all over the table. He struggled to his feet, apologising like mad, and stumbled to the bathroom. There, he emptied his guts a second time, and came out of the cubicle to find Asif waiting. Asif handed him a fistful of paper towels.

Jay turned on the water. "Sorry, man," he said.

"Happens to the best of us. What happened?"

"System upgrade," Jay said. "But what the hell? I'm awake!"

"It seems unlikely, yeah."

"You know anyone named Billy?" Jay asked, and told Asif about the zips. The code had an unfamiliar prefix.

"Wonder who he is?" Jay mused.

Asif's milky eye blinked more slowly than the healthy one. "Have you thought...this Billy might be, you know, an old contact."

"So... leftovers?" The thought creeped Jay out. Someone else's files in his head? A memory struggled to surface. He felt queasy again. "Fuck! I knew it was too good to be true."

"Geez, man, cheer up!" Asif said, watching Jay wretch. "You puked in a public place, your system's a bit glitchy, so what? Your day's been way better than mine.

42

Some woman in Bangladesh diverted my call to the local privacy commission: that was a fun two hours. You probably just need to defrag, run a full scan, and that'll be it." Asif pursed his lips. "But you might want to do it at home. You go back to work smelling like that, that'll be the end of your love life. And what's with your neck?"

Jay peered into the mirror. He'd fouled the front of his graduation shirt, but what Asif had noticed was an angry rash blooming from the open collar. He touched it. The skin was rough, slightly itchy. He rubbed at it. Hives?

Jay took Asif's advice, called in sick and went home. He meant to do the defrag right away, but first it was a dose of antihistamine to stop the itching. Then, he got a zip that the new season of *Devil in Blue* had just been released, so he settled down to watch that. Then in *KopyKat* things were getting really interesting with a player Jay had been hanging with for a few days and it was going to take a few rounds' game-time to even things out, so obviously, that had to be taken care of. Then, the antihistamine making him drowsy, he nodded off.

the eyes have it

The defrag just slipped his mind.

*

Jay arrived at work the following Monday feeling like he was on the cusp of something pretty damn cool. He'd wakened Saturday morning feeling better, the rash having receded to pale dots on his stomach and thighs. In the shower, he'd decided that the violet eyes gave him an edge requiring something other than jeans and a t-shirt. His baby blues had been happy shopping in *True Value*, but the new pair wanted something classier. So, Jay went to *Walmart* and bought flat-fronted pants with just a bit of a sheen and a button-down shirt that flowed off his shoulders like water. He'd added shoes with enough of a heel so his altitude felt right. He liked the way the pants and the shirt and the shoes made him walk. Then he and Asif had gone out.

It had been a great night. They had gone from a coffee pub to a booze pub to a dance pub. Jay's violet eyes, flashy clothes, and his new swagger -- a change Asif was not sure he liked -- had men and women alike zipping

44

him their short codes. Jay had sent a polite 'Ignore' to each one, and the men and the women, who'd seen him come in with Asif, thought Asif was a really lucky guy.

It had been a great weekend. Jay took his coffee from the dispenser (he'd asked Alice to change it from double-double to cream-no-sugar) and settled into his chair. For the first time, Jay saw not only exactly how the rest of his life was going to go, but how he was going to get there.

He was a new Jay, a new man. This morning he was going to zip Sandra and ask her out on a date, a real one, not virtual. Mark the calendar, my friends, today was the first day of the rest of Jay Chadha's life. He toggled Sandra's avatar.

His vision greyed out. The room spun. A countdown appeared in the bottom left-hand corner of his visual field.

Jay blinked it away, but it remained.

11:59:46

"What the hell?"

the eyes have it

Jay put his coffee down and accessed his system trouble-shooter. It worked away for a second or two and then told him nothing was wrong.

"Like hell there's nothing wrong," Jay said, and remembered the defrag. He still hadn't gotten around to doing it. He'd better do it now. He posted a virtual 'do not disturb' sign and initiated a low-level privacy screen which suggested he was on the line with a potentially big customer. The defrag was quick: the news and adverts on the walls of his cubicle went transparent as computing power was briefly committed to housekeeping. The scan took longer. The headache ballooned throughout his skull and then the pain receded, leaving a blinking icon in the centre of his vision.

VIRUS DETECTED

And 437 828 messages lit up his inbox. All from Billy.

"Fuck!" Karim had said he was clean. Jay zipped a form complaint to Karim and looked for his anti-virus. That icon was missing. Of course. Jay initiated a search and came up goose eggs. The anti-virus program was gone from his system. Huffing in frustration, Jay accessed Alice.

"Yes, Mr. Chadha?" Alice said.

"I've picked up a virus," Jay said. "Contain and eradicate."

"Please wait."

Jay's vision greyed as Alice accessed his ware. It took no time at all. The countdown timer disappeared. "Thanks, Alice," Jay said.

"You have a message," Alice said.

"Play it for me," Jay said, taking down the privacy screen and the 'do not disturb' icon.

"Message reads," Alice said, "You have 11:49:22 hours."

Goosebumps lifted the hairs on Jay's arms. The damn virus had gotten into the A.I. and Karim hadn't responded to his complaint. He sent another and added a priority tag. A head poked over the top of his cubicle: Sandra.

"Your display okay?" she asked him. "Mine just conked out on me."

"What do you mean, 'conked out'?" Jay said.

"Look." Sandra sent a copy of her display to Jay's wall. There were three numbers on it: 11:48:39. "It's counting down," Sandra added. "What do you think it means?"

"No idea," Jay said, feeling as if ice water had just landed in his lap. He heard Nakroo complaining across the aisle, and then there was a general shuffle as Jay's colleagues popped out of their cubicles like groundhogs sniffing for danger.

"It's happening all over," Sandra observed. Then she frowned. "My server's down. Oh." She grinned. "I'm back on-line." She looked at Jay. "You have 11:48:09 hours."

"Jesus!" Jay exclaimed, falling back out of his chair. He crab-scrambled out of his cubicle and found his feet. Ben looked at him, and Nakroo. Sandra had developed a frown line between her brows and followed him as he got to his feet and backed down the aisle.

"Jay?"

One by one, the building emitters flickered to the running countdown until every surface Jay looked at ticked down. Jay stumbled down the hallway and the elevator door opened for him. "Ground floor," he gasped, heart pounding. He called Karim, direct video link with a PANIC attachment and kept the line open while it rang. And rang. And rang. The elevator reached the ground floor. Jay straightened up, tried to look collected and calm as the doors opened. His head was pounding. The countdown flashed at him from the lobby ceiling and walls. Jay made a bee-line for the exit.

Karim answered. "What the hell is wrong with you?" Karim demanded. Karim was pulling a shirt over his head. "What in hell you hit the panic button for?"

"Virus," Jay said quickly. "It's infected my company's A.I. You said they were clean!" Jay exited the building and followed the signs for the pedway. The door slid shut behind him. Jay scanned the walls around him, the sidewalks, the store windows. Everything looked normal. Ads for coffee, fast food and the latest gadgets. On a huge adboard above the street a mojo dancer advertised KopyKat. Then there was a burst of static and all the emitters cleared. There was a shimmer, and the countdown appeared. "It's in the city system, Karim!"

The silver sheen of Karim's top-of-the-line eyes flickered over the video link. "You called me?" he said. "Shit!"

"Don't hang up!" Jay spoke out loud. A woman passing him in the street gave him a look. "I need a diagnostic!"

"I'm not accessing your system if you're infected," Karim said. Jay recognized the shouting-down-a-tunnel sound as Karim threw up firewalls. "What about your anti-virus? I copped that directly from CSIS. It's a thing of beauty."

"It's not there," Jay said, struggling to think through the headache and his panic. "When I had the company's A.I. have a go, it got infected, and then I think it got into my co-worker's system. And my head! It's killing me. There's a major fuck-up happening here."

"Damn," Karim breathed. "Sounds like a plague rat." Jay stumbled down the ramp of the sloway. In three transfers and he would be on the quickway headed for Karim's place. This time of the day, the sloway was all but empty. Jay fell into a seat. "You're not coming here," Karim said. Of course, he was tracking him. "Not with that virus on board."

"You have to take care of this," Jay said.

"Not my problem, buddy," Karim said.

"You put it in me!" Jay exclaimed.

"Sorry," Karim said. "Listen, I'm going to zip you the code for a special cache of mine. I'll dump a copy of that anti-virus in there, coded to you. Got it? Run it through your system, then restart. That should do it."

"No way, Karim," Jay said. He hated the whine he heard in his voice. The sloway picked up his preferences, displayed a short list of vids Jay might enjoy, then, with a flicker, replaced them with the countdown. What the hell was going on? "There's been nothing but problems since the replant. This was on your watch, man. You've got to fix it."

The zip landed in Jay's inbox.

"You're not coming here, buddy. Don't call me again." Karim's voice began to fade, Doppler-like, as he threw a Chameleon net out to protect his system from Jay's. "It's too big a risk."

Karim severed the link.

Jay slumped back into his seat. He'd only had the system for six weeks! Next time, Jay promised himself, next time he was going to do what everyone else did: max out his credit, borrow from his pension, whatever it took.

Next time, he would buy off the shelf.

Jay almost changed direction. He was about to transfer when he changed his mind. What would new Jay do? He pulled his feeds in one by one and instructed all but his most essential systems to hibernate. Without his own system broadcasting, he was less likely to infect the systems around him. The headache faded, but the rash had returned, and the countdown remained in his POV and on the walls of the sloway: 11:28:32. Karim's zip stared at him, splayed open on his cortex, the link shimmering nauseatingly.

At 11:02:53, Jay was standing in front of Karim's brownstone, pounding on the door with his fist. "I know you're there!" Jay hollered. People stared at him. Jay didn't care. "You put this in me and you got to fix it!" Truth was, if Karim didn't let him in, Jay didn't know what he was going to do. He pounded at the door again. "Let me in or I'll zip this thing to you direct!" Jay shouted, feeling inspired. "I'll broadcast it to your whole frigging neighbourhood!"

"Hey," a voice said.

Jay turned. There was a guy behind him, hands in pockets, smiling benignly.

"What?" Jay said. His hand was throbbing from hitting the door.

"This is going to hurt," the guy said with a shrug. He took his hands from his pocket and punched Jay squarely on the chin.

*

The house looms behind him. He's royally pissed off. It's been a shit of a day.

Jay opened his eyes. Sparks of pain flared out from his jaw.

"Rob hit you," Karim said. He was sitting beside Jay, a tangle of wires running across his lap which were attached to an antique piece of hardware.

"Sorry." A shadow moved and resolved into the man who had hit Jay. "But you were being an asshole."

"What's going on?" Jay managed at last. He tasted the tang of blood. The countdown, he noticed, was still ticking away: 10:38:07

"You got a virus," Karim said. "A nasty one."

"I know that," Jay said. "Your anti-virus worked great, by the way, thanks a lot."

"Sorry about that," Karim said. It sounded like he almost meant it, but he still had not looked at Jay. He tapped at something, and Jay realised he was using an actual keyboard, which meant the hardware was an actual computer.

"What is this?" he asked.

"We've gone Old School," Karim said. "About the only smart thing you did today was turn off your Wifi. I'm hoping..." tap, tap, tap... "that this dinosaur can find out what in hell is going on with you. Shit, man, would you lie still?"

Jay considered not doing as Karim had asked, but Rob crossed his arms and took a step closer. The man looked even bigger in Karim's apartment than he had on the street. Jay lay back down.

"Your anti-virus has been deleted," Karim said.

"Not by me."

"I can see that," Karim said. "I want to know who did. I don't see any sign of unauthorised access, no hacking traces, but why would anyone hack you anyway? You're no one."

"Thanks."

"Be grateful," Rob said. "Being someone ain't that great."

"How would you know?' Karim said, but he said it with a smile that made Jay reassess their relationship.

"Who are you, anyway?" Jay asked Rob.

Rob shrugged. "I'm his supplier."

Jay blinked. "What? Drugs?"

Karim snorted a laugh. Rob grinned. "Yeah, sure," he said. "Drugs."

Karim beckoned to Rob. "Check this out."

Rob frowned at the screen. "What am I looking at?"

"It's not a virus, exactly, although it acts like one. It's a sneaky little shit, that's for sure. I've heard of them, but never actually seen one. Where'd you get these?"

Rob shrugged. "The usual, babe, it's been a slow season."

Karim frowned. "Okay," he said. "I have something here I can try. It might solve the problem, it might not. Want to give it a go?"

"Oh," Jay said. "You're talking to me now?"

"Cut the attitude," Rob said. "You want his help or not?"

"What do you mean it might solve the problem?" Jay said.

"Just that. Might." Karim's expression was matter-of-fact.

Jay sagged. What choice did he have? He couldn't live like this, and he couldn't afford another pair of eyes. "Whatever," he said. "I just want it gone."

"It'll be rough," Karim warned. Rob plunked a bucket on the floor by the sofa. Karim touched something on the computer.

Jay's head, already tender, erupted in white fire.

System designers had been working on the physical issues of tech and 'ware ever since Nareem Robertson had had the first cumbersome Wifi embedded

57

under his skin back in '19. Infection and system-attacks had been pretty much weeded out by the time Logicorp took their hardware to the free market, but headaches were still an issue. The primitive brain stem protested vehemently against an evolution that happened too quickly for mere flesh to keep pace with. Various solutions had been proposed, the latest one being a sub-dermal factory that injected analgesics directly to the blood stream whenever an upgrade was triggered, or whenever a particularly nasty system cleansing, like the one Karim had just initiated, was enabled.

Jay couldn't afford anything that sophisticated.

Jay squeezed his eyes shut. The vision in his right eye had become distorted, and through it, like needles, the damn countdown still maintained cohesion. Then, there was an explosion of sound. A flurry of images came with it, passing his visual cortex so fast he had no chance to sort one from the other. *He's furious and panting from adrenaline. There's no time to take care of it properly. He'll have to come back.* Then the nausea: most of it in the bucket, Jay hoped. He heaved his guts dry, was left gasping and choking, hanging over the edge of the sofa.

"Ah, hell," he heard Karim say.

"Is that what it looks like?" Rob had come close, despite the mess. Jay could see his black leather shoes.

"It can't be anything else."

"Then he's totally screwed."

"What?" Jay managed, the single word causing more heaving.

"I'm sorry, Jay," Karim said. "It didn't work. He's too deeply embedded. Must be one hell of a death wish with this guy."

"What is it?" Jay struggled upright, a string of mucus dangling from his lower lip. Rob actually looked sorry for him. Karim turned his monitor so Jay could see it. There was a mass of data racing across the screen, illegibly fast, creating flexes of light and shadow. Jay struggled to understand what he was seeing. "That's…" he didn't finish. It sounded stupid.

"A face," Karim finished for him. "You don't have a virus, Jay. What you have, is a ghost."

Jay barked a laugh. "You're kidding."

"I wish I was," Karim said, "but there he is."

"But, that's just zipbait!" Jay exclaimed. "No one believes what they read on the 'net. A ghost! Don't be ridiculous." He looked to Rob.

"Hey," Rob said, "I'm just the help."

"It's like the... the Loch Ness monster. Lots of blurry pictures, but no one actually believes in it. It's bullshit."

"Okay, then," Karim said. He started pulling wires from the computer and tossing them at Jay. "Guess we're done here. Rob? You wanna explain what happens if he shows up here again?"

"Sure thing."

"Wait!' Jay said. "That's it?"

"Yep," Karim said. "I can't do anything for you. So. Fuck off." He yanked the wires from Jay's access hub with a pop.

"You can't just leave me like this," Jay protested. Then he noticed the countdown. It had changed from green to yellow as if it were a warning. Rob took another step closer and Jay struggled to his feet, wiping his mouth with the back of his hand. "I need a new system! I can maybe make a down-payment...." Rob grabbed his shoulder with a huge hand and steered him for the door.

"You're done here," he said.

"No more freebies, Jay," Karim added, "and I don't want your business anymore."

"And a friendly word of advice," Rob added. "I wouldn't open any messages from Billy, if I were you."

"What? Why not?"

"That's the ghost's name: Billy. He's been trying to get in touch."

*

"How many messages?"

"Another 4 000," Jay said glumly, "all from Billy. I'm drowning in here; my whole system is gummed up."

61

the eyes have it

Jay had gone straight from Karim's place to Asif's, and told Asif everything that had happened. Asif had spent half an hour reading up about ghosts, and in conclusion had told Jay that he was well and truly screwed.

"How did it get in my system?" Jay asked, still not sure that 'ghost' wasn't just a cute nickname for a particularly nasty virus.

"It was already in your system. It's a psychic imprint," Asif said. "Before 'ware, ghosts like this imprinted on a place. Now, well, they imprint in 'ware. Makes sense, really, something traumatic happens to a soul, it's going to grab onto the closest object available. 'Ware is in our heads, Jay, it doesn't get much more intimate than that. Your man Billy died unexpectedly, probably violently and in a lot of distress, imprinted the memory of that on his 'ware, some unethical morgue attendant harvested the 'ware, and some poor sucker, you, had it installed."

"How do I get it out?" Jay asked. "I can't live like this, man, not again!"

"Well," Asif said, "it says here that the best thing to do is find out what it wants. Yeah, cut it out with the eye rolling, okay?"

"What could it possibly want?" Jay said, pressing his fingers to the bridge of his nose. He'd raided Asif's medicine cabinet, but the drugs weren't taking the edge off the pain. It made thinking difficult. "It's a ghost."

Asif thought for a second, and then raised a finger. "A ghost can get stuck here if it's got unfinished business, yeah? There was that episode of *I Want To Believe*, remember? The one with the ghost?"

"The *one* with the ghost?" Jay said. "Could you be a bit more specific? I have a time limit." The countdown continued to run down. There were under nine hours left. Jay had no idea of what would happen when the countdown ran out, but he sure as hell did not want to find out. *There's a house. A hedgerow.*

"The ghost couldn't pass on to the next plane of existence until it had finished its business. So Marly, the hero, right? Marly lets the ghost take possession of his body, just for a night, and the ghost makes love to the wife one last time and she gets pregnant from it, because she always wanted children but the ghost was like, infertile, or something." Asif was grinning. "That was a really good episode," he said.

"That doesn't sound so bad," Jay admitted. "How did Marly find out what the ghost wanted?"

"He lit a white candle, I think," Asif said.

"You got candles?"

"Or," Asif said, "you could try opening one of his messages. You said he was trying to get in touch."

"They said not to."

Asif sat back, arms wide. "What do you want to do, man? It's your call."

Jay buried his head in his hands. He'd had it all, finally, he'd had it! The system, a job he was good at, a girl who liked him. And now this. Why did things like this always happen to him?

"What are your options?" Asif said.

What options? Jay couldn't go to a doctor: he'd be charged, have his system confiscated and be worse off than a Natural. Karim had made it pretty clear he wasn't welcome there, and it would be months before he had enough money together for even his own set of eye-buds. Not that he could work like this, so making money was going to be a bit of a trick. He supposed he could go to his dad, but their relationship wasn't the greatest since Jay had said exactly what he thought of his father's girlfriend. There weren't any options.

"So," he said, "you think opening one of the messages is a good idea?"

"Fuck, man, this is the twenty-first century. Makes more sense than lighting a damn candle."

"Okay. Here I go," Jay said. He picked the most recent and toggled it open.

It was a series of images. A street. A house. A lump of something in a hedgerow. A street. A house. A lump.

"It's on a loop," Jay said, explaining what he saw. "That's it? Three images?" Then he felt it. *He was furious. What in fuck had that little shit been thinking? And now this? Now this? There was no time. He'd have to come back later. The little shit! The stupid, selfish, shit!*

"Whoa!" Asif exclaimed. "What the hell?"

Jay realised he'd been shouting. He wiped the spit from his mouth.

"What the hell was that, man?"

Jay didn't know. He was shaking, his heart was pounding. For a moment, just a moment, he thought he'd had hold of something, he'd thought he'd been squeezing... squeezing. The muscles in his arms ached.

Billy?

"Who the hell was this guy?" Jay whispered, aghast. What was in his head?

"Show me the message," Asif said, digging a small quick drive from a drawer. Jay fobbed the images into the quick drive and plugged it into Asif's emitter.

"I'll try an image match," Asif said. He captured the image with his good right eye and sent a request to his system. "There's a street sign here, and the house has a number. You might be lucky."

They waited less than a minute. "Good sir," Asif told Jay, "we have a destination."

*

Google narrowed the blurry street sign down to twelve possibilities, only two of which were in the province. And only one of those was in a neighbourhood which matched the other pictures, so Asif was feeling quite the detective when he ordered a long-range taxi to meet them when they got off the quickway.

"I could be a P.I.!" Asif said when he and Jay left the quickway at the edge of the intown vehicular zone. He got into the waiting cab. "You coming?" Jay walked like a man in a dream, the bruise along his jaw line having coloured spectacularly. The rash had returned, too, and Jay scratched at it absently.

It was a long drive through the suburbs, but once the cab cleared the no-congestion zone it slipped into the HOV lanes of the cross-town and accelerated, past the once-fashionable mega-towers of the early part of the century, through abandoned industrial estates that only now were being revived into family-friendly theme parks and then, at last, into the superurbs, those ever into-and-out of style neighbourhoods which were neither of the city, nor of the heavily protected and by-lawed country-side.

The cab glided to a silent halt at a pedestrian quickway. Asif paid. Jay, shut down, was helpless as a Natural. His system countdown still ticked away. When Jay had asked Asif to call in sick to work for him, a temporary A.I. interface had informed them that Holdings PLC was on shut-down until further notice. He'd asked Asif to zip Sandra, but she'd not returned the message.

On the up side, Billy had stopped sending messages.

Jay and Asif changed to the sloway at Richmond, hopped the line at Magnolia Trail, and within the hour they were standing under the same street sign Billy's message had shown them. "Winding Ridgeway", the sign declared, and the street did, indeed, wind a little up a hill and around a corner.

"Reminds me of when we were kids," Asif said. "Look at the street."

The street had yet to be reclaimed here, and there was even a faded yellow line down the centre which divided one side of the street from the other. The houses, what was left of them, were immense, their front yards little more than paved areas for parking cars.

"My grandparents lived in a neighbourhood like this," Asif said, stepping out onto the street. "We used to go there when we were kids. We weren't allowed to play out front because Mom was afraid we'd get hit by a car. Hey. You okay?"

69

Jay had gone completely white.

"Shit, man, you okay?"

"I don't know, I don't know," Jay muttered, half to himself. "It's like a reboot, or something." Just there, just for a moment, his vision had blacked out. It had returned, almost as quickly, but there was a sense of distance about him now, and Asif's voice was coming from a very long way away. He felt cold, cold, cold.

"Stay with me, man," Asif said, taking Jay by the elbow. "You need to help me find the place."

"Yeah." Jay smoothed the front of his shirt. Half the houses were in ruins, brick veneer peeling off in strips and chunks, swollen plywood black with mould, asphalt cracked and spouting green. Some few were still lived in, but the storage pods sitting in the driveways of those houses said that their days were numbered, too. At the bottom of the street, an artistic grouping of construction equipment waited the end of a latest strike action. Behind the equipment, smooth blank lots awaited their next transformation. In front of them, empty foundations, cleared of environmentally dangerous material, waited to be filled in. In half a year, provided the Union managed to get back-to-work legislation put in place, new live-and-work communities would stand here: intensive-use green spaces, independent solar power and ecological responsibility. It was an environmentalist's wet dream.

"There," Jay said, pointing to the house at the end of the row. That was the one, he was sure of it. Yes. There was the hedge, an overgrown tangle of something which had once marked the boundary between two monster homes. On the other side of the hedge, a yellow digger sat idle, partway through filling in a newly-made-illegal swimming pool.

"Yes!" Asif said, pulling Jay along the street. "Now where?"

"The hedge," Jay muttered, but there was a knot of anxiety in his gut. He stopped. "Who do you think this Billy is, anyway?" he asked.

Asif shrugged. "Does it matter?" he said.

"Maybe, yeah," Jay said. "I mean, look at this place."

Asif did. "It does have a kind of slasher flick vibe going on," he admitted. "But, hell, it's broad daylight. What could go wrong?"

All Jay knew was that when he looked at the street, especially at the corner, there, where they'd gotten off the sloway, he felt like he had to take a piss real bad. There was light. Then dark. Deep, deep dark.

Asif's hand was under his elbow again. "Let's just get it done, okay?" he said.

Jay nodded. "Over there." He pointed. At the bottom of the old yard, where the hedge came up against a swale full of muddy water, there was a lump of earth.

"Hey, do you think it could be a sack of money?" Asif whooped and clapped Jay on the shoulder. "Are we gonna be rich, man?" There was a length of 2x4 lying on the ground. Asif trotted over and picked it up. "Hey!" he laughed, "if it is money, won't Karim be pissed? Come on!"

Jay's stomach was uneasy, but he followed Asif to the mound. Jay could see where the dirt had been piled when the hole had been dug. It was pretty obvious something had been buried, but it was equally obvious it had been done in a rush.

"Worst hiding job ever," Asif said poking the mound with his stick. "I'd have hid my money better, if I was him. Still, makes it easier for us!"

"Uh, Asif..." Jay said, suddenly feeling really unhappy. Asif gave the mound a real jab. There was a sucking noise.

"Gah!" Asif reared back, flinging an arm over his face. The scent hit Jay like a wall, dense, cloying, burning. Jay scrambled away, pulling his shirt up over his nose and mouth.

"Gah!" Asif exclaimed again. He ran past Jay, almost pushing him over.

Jay tried to speak, then gagged. He ran after Asif. "Where you going? Shit!" Jay rejoined Asif on the street. Asif's face had gone white.

"I don't even want to know what the hell that is!" Asif exclaimed. "Fuck Billy! Fuck! That's the most disgusting thing I've ever smelled." He sniffed the back of his hand. "Geez, it's on me."

"It's like something died," Jay said.

Then they both fell silent. Jay straightened, eyes fixed on the mound. Asif looked at Jay.

"Ah, hell, no," Asif said. Jay pulled his arms across his chest, began backing away. "You're kidding, right? Tell me you're kidding!" Jay turned and ran the way they'd come. Asif shouted after him, "You'd better be bloody kidding!"

*

They found a Tim Hortons and fortified themselves with double-doubles.

"That's him," Jay said. There was an image on the table emitter of a white guy in his fifties, fleshy, red-faced, and broad-shouldered. "What does it say about him?"

Asif fed the result back into his system. He paled. "Well, this sure sucks," he said. "We should have looked him up way sooner."

"Just tell me."

"Three months ago William "Billy" Bennett Bentham, age 46, died of a brain aneurysm getting onto the quickway at... ready for this?... Magnolia Trail. The police got involved because Bentham's system was stolen from his body before a post mortem could be conducted. Police now also suspect Bentham might have been involved in the disappearance of Peter James Anderson, that guy who's missing. You've seen the newsfeeds, right?"

"Maybe. The name's familiar."

"Bentham and Anderson were known to do business, and Bentham was thought to be connected with the same family that owns FarCom."

"Oh." That name he knew. They owned most of the province, had most municipal politicians in their pockets. They were a scary bunch.

Asif leaned forward, whispered. "If that's Anderson lying there, why in hell didn't Billy do a better job getting rid of the body? It's going to be found, right? As soon as those diggers move in. That smell? They can't miss it!" Asif's voice faded, and his eyes widened. Jay's heart thumped as he got it, too.

"He didn't have time," Jay guessed, feeling the headache build again. The countdown pulsed in his POV. "He meant to go back."

"But he died before he could," Asif said. "Shit."

"That's the unfinished business," Jay whispered. "That's it."

The countdown turned to red.

"To hell with this," Asif said. "This has nothing to do with us. This is cop business. I say we call them through a street hub, let them know what we found, and then bugger off. They don't need to know anything about us, and we can just go home."

"What about me?" Jay said. "I can't live like this!"

"You can learn," Asif said. "Shit, man, you did it before, it wasn't that bad, was it? Just say your system bugged. That happens."

"I can't." His system had begun a slow cascade since they'd run from the house. Jay didn't even bother requesting his system for a diagnostic. "I can't live like that again." His heart began to pound at the thought. Not again. Fuck being a charity case.

"So what do you want to do? You want to go dig up a dead guy? That's fucked, man! I don't have any issue with replants, but a complete corpse is just a bit too far."

"It's okay, Asif. You don't have to do this. This is my problem, and I'll figure it out. You've done more than enough already."

Asif sat back. His expression softened. "You sure?"

"Sure," Jay said. "Just, one more thing, okay?"

They found a hardware store and purchased Vaseline, heavy duty drop sheet, a shovel and a wheelbarrow. Now they stood outside the store awkwardly.

"All right?" Asif said, hands in pockets.

"Yep."

The light was lowering. Asif had argued for waiting until well after sunset, but Jay didn't want to be stumbling around in the dark. He'd had this sudden image of stepping on something soft and ripe. Something he couldn't see.

"Remember what I said," Asif said, tossing the small jar of Vaseline to Jay.

"I can't imagine this will help," Jay said. He popped the lid off and smeared a generous amount under his nose and over his top lip. "It's disgusting."

"It sure can't hurt," Asif said. "How will you do this if you're too busy hurling your guts out? I'll see you at Tim's, you know, after."

Jay rubbed his temples. His vision had gone off, like the saturation had been tampered with.

"You okay?" Asif said.

"I've gone Natural, I think," Jay said, rubbing his eyes. They blurred rather than pixelated. "Yep."

"Shit," Asif said. "Can you even see?"

"I said Natural, not blind," Jay shot back.

"Sorry." Asif offered his hand, and they shook.

It was easy to be cool about the whole thing while on your third double-double in a warm Tim's. But now Jay was pushing a wheelbarrow with a shovel and tarpaulin in it down the street toward the last house. In the dim light, the diggers at the bottom of the street looked like they might come alive. They loomed over what had once been a neighbourhood of huge houses and three-car garages.

"Let's just do this," Jay muttered to himself, advancing toward the mound with the tarp held in front of him like a shield.

The 2x4 pointed at the mound as if to remind them where he'd left off. Jay sniffed the air. The smell was still there, and though it bunched up in the back of his throat, it wasn't nearly as bad as it had been earlier.

the eyes have it

Jay glanced around to make sure there was no one about. He was in the shadow of the house. The hedge blocked the view of the construction site. There were some lights a few blocks over, but they were sparse. The new neighbourhood was a ways from being finished; there was no one about. Jay unrolled the tarp alongside the mound lengthwise and began unfolding it. A slight breeze instantly caught it and flung it back over itself.

Jay hunted around in the half-dark and came up with three good-sized stones. He laid the tarp flat again and weighed it down with the stones. He was already puffing, and that was just from getting the plastic sorted. The breeze was a pain. The good thing, though, was that it was blowing away from him, so now there was hardly any smell at all. The mound was simply a dark shadow. With luck, he wouldn't really even see anything, either. He stood there a moment with the shovel. He had an overwhelmingly good feeling all of a sudden, like he could do anything he set his mind to.

He'd bought a spade, reasoning that the long flat blade would be the most useful. Jay liked the heft of it in his hands. He liked the shine of the sharp edge. Now it was just a matter of just hoisting the... well, Jay still hadn't quite come to terms with calling it a body. It was just a matter of shunting the thing over onto the tarp. Jay put the edge of the shovel beside the mound, placed his foot on the shoulder and stepped down. The blade cut about three centimetres into the earth and jammed.

A rock. Jay repositioned the shovel. It was hard to get at the shoulder from this angle. The plastic was in the way. He shoved it aside with his foot and tried again. This time, the shovel went in easily, right up to the shoulder.

Jay pushed down on the shovel. There was an instant when he thought it wasn't going to move, but then the shovel gave way, there was a sucking sound, and a massive smell of rotting meat sprang into the air.

Jay dropped the shovel and ran, throwing up as he ran, splashing regurgitated coffee-with-cream down his trouser legs. He stopped before he got to the street this time, came up panting and spitting against the side of the condemned building. The smell had followed him, clinging to his hair and his clothes. Jay found himself almost grateful for the odour of vomit.

"Forget it," Jay gasped. "It's not worth it. Nothing is worth this."

"I got your back, man."

"Asif!" Jay had never been so happy to see anyone in his life.

Asif had smeared his lower face with Vaseline. It made him look like he'd sneezed his sinuses clear. "What kind of friend would I be if I left this to you?"

Jay shook his head. "No, you were right. This is for the police."

"Then what happens to you? Cops'll confiscate your system. You'll lose your job for sure, and you haven't even spoken to that Sandra yet, have you?"

"So what?" Jay said, sinking to the ground.

"This isn't your fault, man," Asif said. "You just got stuck with a shitty situation."

"I've been invisible before," Jay said. "I can do it again."

"Screw that. You think I want to hang with some freaking Natural?" Asif began marching toward the body, pulling his shirt off and wrapping it over his mouth and nose like it was a scarf. "I'll do it. You stay here."

Asif grabbed the shovel from where Jay had dropped it, kicked the sheet under the leading edge of the mound, squeezed around between it and the hedge, and jammed the shovel into the ground. He got the mound shifted, dark earth cascading off what lay just underneath, but it was heavy and loose. It simply wasn't a one-man job.

Next thing Jay knew, he was standing beside his friend. He took the shovel from him.

"So I figure," he said, "that if I, you know, lift it on one side with the shovel, you can tuck the plastic in underneath. Then we can just sort of roll it up." He jammed the shovel under the body and pushed down.

Something gleamed at him wetly. Jay closed his eyes, heaved again. Air leaked from between his lips.

Suddenly it moved. Jay risked a look. Asif had the 2x4 jammed against the body. "Now!" Asif said, and they heaved together. The body came free, rolled toward the plastic sheet, and stopped, half on, half off.

"Whoof!" Jay exhaled, threw his arm up over his face and took a breath, choking.

"Come on," Asif grunted. "Almost there." He jammed the wood under the body. Jay went in with the shovel. They heaved the body over once more, eyes averted, and when it stopped moving and they chanced a peek, it was, mostly, lying on the plastic.

"Now roll it up, roll it up!" Jay said, and they grabbed opposite ends of the plastic. Easier said than done. The body was a good size, and uncooperative, and it preferred to slosh on the plastic rather than roll into a neat bundle. Jay got his side covered over, then Asif did his, and then, using the shovel, they managed to get it to flop over again, and when the ends were folded over, it was mostly sealed in.

"When this is done," Asif said. "I'm going to shower for a week."

"Come on," Jay said.

The rolling up went a little faster now that it was started. Asif insisted on using the shovel at first but it was sharp and threatened to tear the plastic. Finally, reluctantly, the two of them knelt beside the body and heaved it over and over with their hands, trying very hard not to think about the soft giving beneath the tarpaulin.

"I don't think I could do this if it was still warm," Asif said conversationally.

Jay nodded, "Like a burrito," he said.

"Hunh?" Asif said.

"It if it was warm," Jay clarified, "it would be like rolling a burrito."

Asif's eyes went wide, and he cracked a smile.

"Sorry," Jay said. "Couldn't help it." And he smiled, too, and that turned into a laugh. Asif joined in, and he looked like such a total zek with his shirt over his face that Jay laughed even harder.

"God, I needed that," Jay said when he could.

"Me, too," Asif said. "You know, I was thinking that when we get done here, if you're system gets sorted, you should book some time from work and we should get tickets for Comicon. What do you think?"

They'd been talking about doing that for ages, but never actually gone. "We should totally do that." As Jay said it, he lost all sight in his left eye. The countdown read 0:40:12. "We should get moving."

Together they levered the body into the wheelbarrow. It was heavier than they had thought it would be, and Jay, with only one eye, was having trouble with his balance. Asif offered to push the barrow, and they cut across the old yards toward the half-filled swimming pool.

Jay dug first. The soil was loose enough that Jay left footprints in it and the digging was easy. Asif sat on the edge, legs dangling, one hand on the wheelbarrow.

When Jay's right eye blinked out at 0:15:00, he dropped the shovel and Asif helped him out of the hole. Asif took over. When he figured he had the hole deep enough to completely cover the body, he climbed out and manoeuvred the wheelbarrow.

"Want to say goodbye?" he asked Jay.

"Just do it."

Asif tilted the barrow up. The body seemed to hang on for a moment, then began to slide, then toppled out and landed, with a thump, practically right in Asif's trench.

"Good one," Asif said, continuing his play-by-play. He jumped back into the pool and kicked the body into a better position, then began shovelling dirt over it. "I think it's fine," he said. "I think we're done here, don't you? Man, I hope this is good enough for Billy. The bastard."

The countdown went to 0:00:00, and Jay's system went dark.

*

the eyes have it

Bright light. Blinding. Then darkness. And in that darkness, something moved.

It was hard to say exactly what it was. A figure, maybe, but it was indistinct like something seen through murky water. Gradually, it coalesced into a rainbow pixilation. It formed a suggestion of two legs, two arms, and a vague blob which was an approximation of a head with two empty pits where the eyes would have been, if those eyes had not been taken. It fluttered about at the edge of Jay's knowing, then turned a steady regard to him. Jay stilled. He expected to feel fear. He did not. It was just a man, after all. Flawed, imperfect, groping in the dark like everyone, but still, essentially, a man.

Billy?

There was a tugging. It hurt, exquisitely. When the pain was done, there was such a feeling of loss that Jay wanted to cry out: Wait! Something eased open, something unseen, and Billy slipped away with a sigh. Jay wanted to follow! Oh, he wanted to follow! But he couldn't find the way, and Billy had left no sign but that sigh, and a wondrous, astonishing, letting go.

Jay was left alone in the dark.

*

Jay opened his eyes, *his eyes*, and he wasn't alone. Asif was with him.

"You going to be okay, man?" Asif asked.

Jay's system beeped at him and began running a painless diagnostic. All green.

"Yeah," he told Asif. "I think so."

He raised his hand, and Asif lifted him to his feet.

If you liked what you read, would you take a minute and leave a review at Amazon or Goodreads? Reviews mean the world to writers, and I read every review I get. The best way to support authors you enjoy (other than by reading their books) is by sharing and reviewing. Thank you!

You can find me at **jessicaveter.com**, on Twitter **@jsveter** or on Facebook at **J.S. Veter, Author**.

For occasional updates and free stories, please sign up at **jessicaveter.com**

All seventeen-year-old Jazz Fischer wanted for graduation was a ticket, for one, to England. It was a battle convincing her father, but she did it, and now she is on her own in Jolly Old.

And she's just been hit by a motorcycle. David, who was hit with her, cannot walk. Jazz must find help for them both. Luckily, there is a house not far down the road.

It's hardly Jazz's fault that the people who live there think she's their daughter. Nor is it her fault that David disappears.

What is her fault is what happens to her cousin.

A holiday in England seemed the perfect way to practice being grown up. But for Jazz, practice is over. Something is coming.

Can't you feel it?

Available in paperback or ebook from Amazon or contact info@shoestringhouse.ca

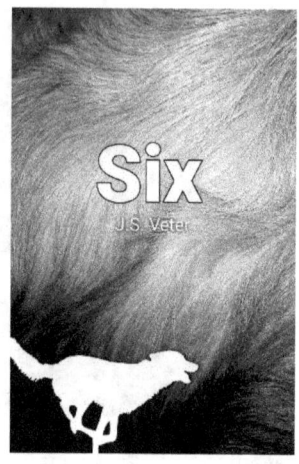

"Welcome to The Bestiary! Unusual Pets for Unusual People since 1890!"

In *The Bestiary*, the rats have started a circus, Bertie the crow gives lectures on living with humans, and Blue the macaw, who understands English, has just been elected Speaker for the Parliament of Fowls.

All the animals in *The Bestiary* have a talent. All the animals, that is, except for Six.

Available in paperback or ebook online or contact info@shoestringhouse.ca